Katarina's Spelling Bee

Written by Al Ulsrud

Illustrated by Lacey Patterson

Katarina

and the Spelling Bee

Introduction

Have you ever met a child who loves to spell and witnessed their joy and triumph when they conquer new words? This next story about Katarina follows her discovery of a new love: spelling. Her curiosity, persistence, and spirit shine through in this educational and fun adventure.

Parents and educators of today's children can see the benefit of balanced learning—developing traditional skills that complement the enticing world of electronic devices. Let Katarina immerse your child and yourself as her vocabulary world expands.

Katarina
and the Spelling Bee

Written by Al Ulsrud

Illustrated by Lacey Patterson

To order additional copies of this book, contact:
Xlibris
844-714-8691
www.Xlibris.com
Orders@Xlibris.com

ISBN: 978-1-6641-2215-4 (sc)
ISBN: 978-1-6641-2216-1 (hc)
ISBN: 978-1-6641-2214-7 (e)

Library of Congress Control Number: 2020914357

Print information available on the last page

Rev. date: 08/20/2020

This book is dedicated to my daughter Katarina, who was my inspiration for this story.

Lacey dedicates her artwork to her friends and family.

In This Series

Katarina's Sleeping Adventure

Spelling bee: *noun*. Perhaps originating in the nineteenth century and likely American, this phrase first appeared in print in 1875.

The term was probably influenced by a gathering of friends and neighbors who came together to help someone in need. These get-togethers were known as sewing bees, quilting bees, or barn raisings. The buzzing insect and the social nature of the beehive could have been another inspiration for the term.

"Hi, Dad," Katarina blurted out as she ran through the door.

"Slow down!" her dad said. "I didn't even hear the school bus stop."

"But I have so much to tell you about school today!"

"OK, sit down first though and take a breath." Her dad handed her a glass of milk and a plate of cookies. "Now what went on in school today?"

"Well," Katarina said. "My teacher surprised us with a new game." She paused, looking at her dad. She had a funny look on her face—she liked to tease her dad sometimes.

"So? Spill the beans, Katarina!"

"First, our teacher told us how important it is to learn to spell, and if we played a game, we would remember better. So she put pieces of paper in a big cup. Each piece had a word on it. Our teacher said some of the words would be tricky. But she said each word would teach us something, and we would discuss it in class. And even better, Dad, she said we should try to use these words in a conversation, which would help us remember."

"Well, what words do you remember?" her dad asked.

So Katarina bounced up and went to her chalkboard to write down a word.

"Dad, you will never get this word! It sounds like this: F-L-E-M." She pointed to her chalkboard. "It's the yucky stuff you clear from your throat!"

"OK, Dad. How do you think it is spelled? It might surprise you!"

He laughed. "It looks fine to me!"

"No, Dad, try to make a guess!"

"Hmm," her dad murmured, trying to figure out the correct way. Then he said, "P-H-L-E-G-M."

Katarina was so surprised. "Dad, you are right! How did you know?"

With a sly grin, he said, "That was one of the first words my dad tried to fool me with. And he did. But I made sure I would never forget that word again." He laughed. "I'll bet you never do either!"

"So what other words did you learn to spell?"

"Well," said Katarina, "there was the word *boo-ee*. It is a bobbing float in the water to warn sailors where they are."

"Did everyone know how to spell that word?" her dad asked.

"No one knew!" Katarina laughed. "So, the teacher told us we should listen carefully to how each of the words is spelled. Then she said there would be a prize for all of us who didn't make a mistake. With this, everyone perked up!"

"What were some of the other words pulled out of the big cup?" her dad asked.

"I won't tell you now." She giggled. "Because I want all of us to play the spelling game after dinner tonight. It will be fun for you, Mom, and Christian."

Her dad said, "That should be fun, but I won't be embarrassed, will I?" He gave her a sly wink.

"No, Dad, you're a smart guy! But let's make it our secret until we have eaten."

Katarina couldn't keep her excitement under control at dinner. She was so bubbly that her mom finally said, "This is either the best meal I've cooked in a long time or, Katarina, you have something up your sleeve."

That evening, after Katarina and her brother, Christian, cleared the dishes, Katarina said to her parents, "Now I want us to play a game."

"Oh, goodie," said Christian. "I love games! What are we going to play?"

"It's a spelling game that I learned at school today. We need to get a cup and some pieces of paper. Christian, can you open the cupboard and get us a cup?"

"Mom, can I have some paper so that I can prepare the words?"

So Katarina spent a few minutes writing down words on pieces of paper that were put in the cup. She then explained the rules of the game. "I will pick a piece of paper from the cup for each of you in turn. I will read the word and its meaning. You will then try to spell it correctly."

"Can I go first? This will be fun!" said Christian.

"Of course, the youngest always goes first," said Katarina as she pulled out the first piece of paper.

She then announced the word to her brother: *bal-lay*.

"Remember when we watched *The Nutcracker* last Christmas? Those were ballet dancers. Can you spell *ballet*?"

B-A-L-L-E-T

Christian thought for a moment then said, "B-A-L-A. Was that right?"

"No, but that was a good try."

"Aww," said Christian, "give me a hint."

"Listen carefully, I'll spell it out slowly. B-A-L-L-E-T. Now try it again, Christian," said Katarina, "and at the same time, think of the ballet dancers."

Christian paused and then uttered, "B-A-L-L-E-T."

"Yay!" said Katarina while her parents smiled.

Katarina then pulled her mom's word from the cup. "Here it is, Mom. It sounds like 'nash.'"

"What's it mean though?" her mom asked.

Katarina replied, "When you grind your teeth like when you're mad sometimes."

Her dad laughed at this, but not her mom, who then paused before spelling the word—"G-N-A-S-H."

"That was great!" Katarina said as her mom gave a grudging smile.

"Now, Dad, here's your word, 'Seezer.' Like the salad."

Her dad slowly answered, "C-A-E-S-A-R."

Christian looked at Katarina and asked, "Is he right?"

"Yes, our parents are both pretty smart!"

"Well, I want to be smart too!" said Christian.

"Then you just need to listen carefully and then memorize," replied Katarina.

Finally, Mom said, "It's getting late. This has been fun, but you have school tomorrow, so off to bed!"

Her dad looked at Katarina as they were cleaning up. "You really like spelling, don't you?"

"Oh yes," she said, "and my teacher mentioned that some people are like a sponge when it comes to remembering words. I think I want to be a word sponge, ha!"

"Well, goodnight, my little sponge," her dad said.

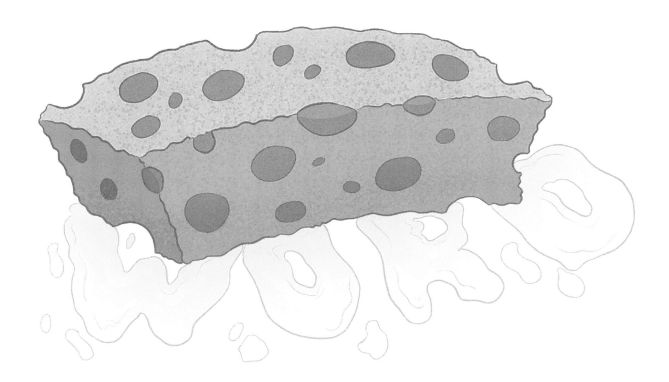

The next afternoon, Katarina ran into the house after the school bus left. She was so excited, and she said to her mom, "Guess what?"

Her mom replied, "Why do I think this is going to be about spelling?"

"You're right, Mom. My friends are coming over here soon. We're going to play spelling bee just like in school."

"Uh-huh," her mom replied. "I bet I know who is going to be the teacher."

Katarina laughed. "You bet! And do I have some good words to test them!"

The house went quiet a bit later, and her mom looked out into the backyard. She could see Katarina in the tree house, standing up and looking at her students.

She slipped out of the house, not wanting to be seen, and walked quietly across the lawn. She listened to Katarina and her friends as new words spilled into the air. She heard *abyss, trolley, choir, mimic, cologne,* and many others as Katarina carefully explained the meaning of the word after she pronounced it. She heard laughs, cheers, and once in a while, a moan.

At dinner later, Katarina told her family, "I've decided I'm going to be a spelling bee teacher."

Her parents smiled, and her mom said, "I think you'll have to teach other subjects too."

Later that evening, Katarina was restless and found herself wandering around the house. She couldn't keep her mind off spelling. Words bounced around her head.

A call from a classmate reminded her that her teacher was going to have a final spelling contest at the end of the week and that there was going to be a special prize!

Katarina had to admit, she liked winning at whatever she tried. Maybe that's why she couldn't sit still. Finally, she thought, *I am going to bed*, as she turned toward the stairs.

Out of the corner of her eye, she spotted her dad sitting in his favorite chair in the living room. She quietly walked up behind him. She peeked over his shoulder and saw that he had a big book in his hands, and it looked familiar. *Gosh*, she thought, *it's a dictionary! What is he doing, reading that book?* As she quietly backed away, she smiled. *I know, he's going to try to find words to trick me with!*

As she climbed the stairs, she informed her family she was going to bed. "Mom, Dad, are you going to tuck me in?"

"We'll be right up after you have brushed your teeth and changed into your pajamas," her mom replied.

After her parents tucked her in, she lay quietly staring at the ceiling. But she couldn't sleep. She smiled and thought, *I know what I'm going to do!*

She quietly slipped out of bed and pulled her top blanket over her headboard and made a sort of tent. With her lantern and a spelling book under the covers, no one could tell she was awake in her dark room.

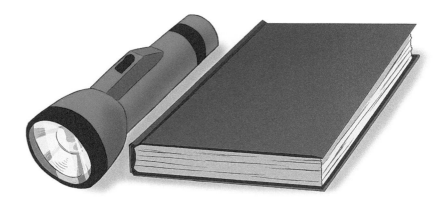

The next morning, Katarina appeared in the kitchen bleary-eyed. Her mom said, "Uh-oh, look who the cat dragged in!"

"That's not funny, Mom. I think I may have studied too late last night."

"I didn't know you had homework."

"No, Mom, you know what I mean. I was practicing spelling different words. Some of them I've never heard before."

"You little monkey, don't you have a final spelling contest in class today? It's a bit late now, but one is always sharper after a good sleep!"

"I know, Mom. But I think I can spell a lot more words now, and the teacher said there would be some tough ones."

Katarina almost fell asleep on the school bus that morning, her head nodding as they approached the school.

In class, she tried to stay alert and smile when her teacher asked her, "Are you all right, Katarina?" At lunch, her friends also noticed that she wasn't as lively as she usually was. Little did they know what was going on in Katarina's mind as she mentally prepared for the afternoon's spelling contest.

When she was finally back in class, the teacher announced, "Now you all know what's coming. It's our final spelling contest! I hope everyone is ready. I know some of you have been preparing," she said, looking at Katarina knowingly.

She continued, "I have prepared all the words, each on a slip of paper in this cup. One after the other, I will pull out your slip of paper and ask you to spell the word after I have told you what it means. Would you all stand next to your desk as I move around the room? If you spell the word wrong, you have to sit down. The last person standing wins!"

As the teacher asked each student to spell their word, she was surprised how well everyone did. In fact, she started to worry that she did not have enough new words in her cup.

Finally, the contest came down to two people—Katarina and one of her good friends, a boy who had practiced with her in her tree house. Her friend went first and was asked to spell *amoeba*. "It's one of the tiniest animals that lives in water," the teacher said.

Oh boy, Katarina thought, *that's a tough one*. Then her friend started to spell the word: "A-M-E-E-B-A."

The teacher frowned slightly and said, "I'm sorry, but that is incorrect."

She then looked at Katarina and said, "Now it's your turn."

Katarina thought, *I've seen this word before somewhere,* so she slowly started to spell the word: "A-M-O-E-B-A."

"That's right, Katarina. You spelled it correctly." There was a murmur in the classroom, followed by clapping. Her friend turned to her and shook her hand with a big smile.

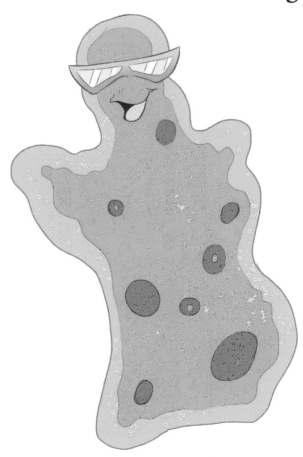

The teacher retreated to the back of her desk and pulled out a book. She opened the front cover and wrote something inside. Then she came over to Katarina and said, "I want to give you this book. It's a classic, and it was my favorite book when I was your age. I know you will enjoy learning the many new words in it."

Katarina smiled broadly. "Thank you very much," she said as she looked inside the cover to see what the teacher wrote.

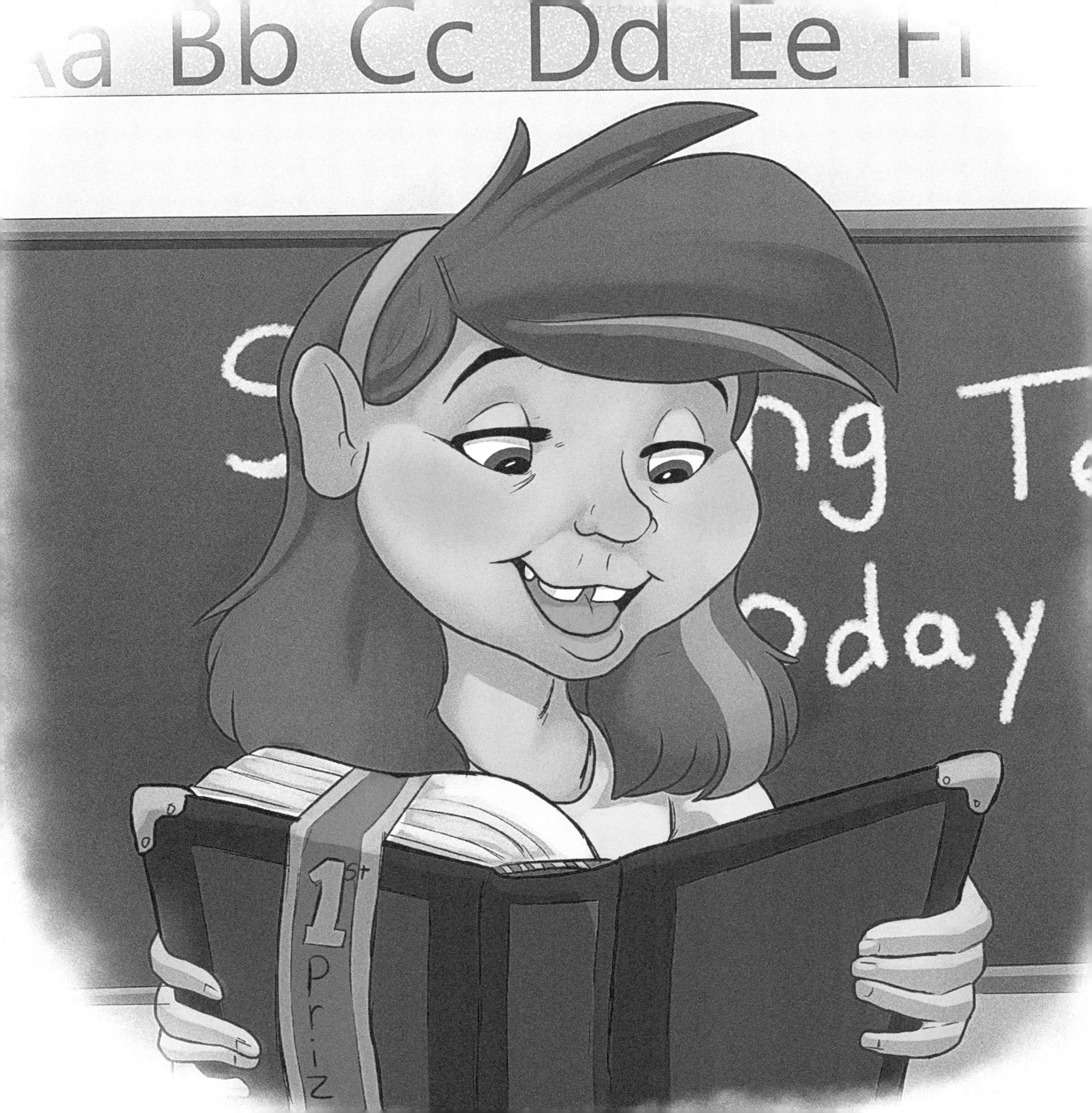
Bb Cc Dd Ee

Katarina could not remember her ride home on the bus that day; she was so excited and couldn't wait to see her family.

To her surprise, her mom, dad, and brother were waiting at the door when she arrived. They yelled, "Surprise!" And her mom held out a big cake.

"Whaaat is this for?"

"Well, we didn't know how your day would go, so we thought, whatever happened with your spelling bee, we couldn't lose if we baked you a cake!"

Katarina laughed and said to her family, "Well, I guess today I'm a double winner! I won the spelling bee!"

She reached into her backpack and pulled out her prize to show them.

Her mother examined the book and then opened the cover and read aloud what the teacher had written.

"Listen to this everyone. 'Dear Katarina, you are a deserving winner of this prize. I love your excitement about new words. You have a very special future. All the best.'"

Dear Katarina,
You are a deserving winner of this prize.
I love your excitement about new words.
You have a very special future.

. All the best.

Her dad and mom exchanged very proud glances, and Christian was beaming. He said, "When are we going to cut the cake?"

That night, her dad announced, "We're going to watch a very special program on TV, but let me keep it a surprise until we sit down later."

With a bowl of freshly popped popcorn in front of them, her dad turned on the TV. Katarina smiled when she realized they were watching the national spelling competition. As the program progressed, she was mesmerized by how smart the contestants were and how complicated the words were.

When she turned to her parents after the program was over, she said, "I'm tired, I'm going to bed."

"Well, it's been a great day for you, Katarina. And tomorrow, I'm going to show you some new words that I've found." Katarina smiled and thought, *I knew he was up to something.*

Then as her mom and dad cleaned up, Christian sat quietly on the sofa. They asked him, "What are you thinking? Aren't you going to bed?"

"Dad, could you show me some tricky words from your dictionary that I could learn?"

"For sure, Christian. Do you think you want to be a spelling champ in the future?"

"Oh yes, especially if I get a cake as a surprise!"

The End

Here's A Quiz!

To Inspired Parents/Teachers:

Katarina has learned the following words as part of her love for spelling. These words can be practiced at bedtime or in the classroom. You'll be pleasantly surprised at how receptive your children are to being challenged with new vocabulary!

Hint: While concealing the list, say the word slowly first, repeating if necessary. Read the meaning. Then ask your child how they think the word is spelled. Remember to be encouraging!

- weird—strange, different
- cemetery—a kind of spooky place
- rhythm—the beat of a song
- arctic—where penguins and polar bears live

- algae—green plants that live in water
- asthma—hard to breathe, can make someone cough
- ancient—really, really old
- dinghy—a little boat
- foreign—from another country or place
- gnome—fairytale person who guards the garden
- disease—sickness
- muscles—help a body move
- ceiling—the top of the room
- queue—the line at the grocery store
- autumn—when the leaves change color
- biscuit—a crunchy treat for the dog
- canoe—a boat to take when camping
- island—land that has water all around it
- mosquito—an annoying little biting insect
- twelfth—the last hour of the day
- tongue—used to lick a lollipop
- knight—wears armor and slays dragons

Al Ulsrud (Author)

In this second book in the series, Katarina discovers the fascinating world of spelling. Her persistence and memory help her meet a very special spelling challenge. From an early age, Al Ulsrud always loved how certain words could convey an undefined feeling in a sentence. He was taught that as a foundation for a diverse vocabulary, correct spelling was important. How a word sounds when spoken often gives little clue to its actual spelling.

Lacey Patterson (Illustrator)

Since the fourth grade, Lacey has been passionate about drawing. Originally pulling inspiration from famous horses, she has explored a variety of art form, from graphic design to cartooning, eventually leading to book illustration. Using art to express herself, she gives every piece a personality that brings the characters to life. This is her second illustrated Katarina book.